Nice People

By

John F King

ISBN
978-0-9931306-6-3

York Europe Publishing

2018

www.johnkinginternational.eu

'Wir wohnten im Paradies -notgedrungen'

L. Marcuse, Sanary 1933-40

Nice People

York Europe Publishing

2018

Contents

ISBN 978-0-9931306-6-3

John F King

www.johnkinginternational.eu

Gare-ish

There is a difference between going back and returning to somewhere you have been to before.

I don't exactly know what it is but there is. Internal tone, perhaps, going back, the futile reworking of receding youth, returning, I like it here, I'll come again.

I wasn't the only one replaying the jingle of the railway platform speakers, the ex-Floyd man had sampled it on a late solo album. I appreciate the company.

The sound was a quad note sequence with a Deneuvian voice.

'Nice Ville, Nice Ville.'

I first came to this city in 1976. The Floyd's line up wasn't that different.

The city hadn't changed beyond its essence, the familiar evening air blend of diesel and bougainvillea.

I like it here, the city by the sea. You can't walk fast and have regrets at the same time. I walk fast.

Avenue Medecin, station at one end, sea at the other, no map required. Nice.

Past Notre Dame, Fnac, Monoprix, Lafayette, improving with every step.

I don't have a favourite café on principle. Keep moving forward, head for the sea, is the only way.

I stop at Massena, the sea will wait for me. I stir the Lipton tea bag vigorously in the non boiling water. I made a comment a long time ago about tea here, now I live with everything.

The trams glide past, their bell more Alp than Maritime. A glass of Mourvèdre would be acceptable.

I never came here for peace, there are quieter places. Usually the Mobylettes are background. Is their foregrounding a change in me? I allow few things to annoy me now, missing a call from you always did unsettle me.

I put the phone on the table next to the second glass – tell you what, leave the bottle, I'll imagine you are with me. Tell you what, I'll drop you a WhatsApp – paper is so passé- make it a call, no it isn't the second glass but you must remember this.

The moped comes out of the sun, two youths, a driver and grabber, the phone is gone, the wine fills the whites on the chequered the table cloth.

How am I going to reach you now?

Belle Epoch

Offer people money. In my experience they will do most things. Not everything. Most things.

Yes, I do have a compass. It's on the yacht.

I have, as you would expect, the best position in the port. To the north bar Le Before, sundowners before landing at the Negresco. To the east Villefranche Menton Monte, to the west Cannes - Tropez, to the south the open sea, not that I want the boat to get wet.

I have the visuals covered. The only *ombre au tableau* is the noise. Directly north, every Sunday morning, the bells, the bells. Church equals problems. I prefer states. Speaking of which Sunday mornings I'm not generally in a state to listen to church bells. I don't appreciate it.

I'm told it is called the Eglise de Notre-Dame-du-Port. I'm told I went in there once, couldn't find my yacht.

Fact: anyone who says they don't want to be rich is lying. I tried not being rich before I was and didn't like it. Money means choice. It doesn't mean everything but the ratio of you choosing things to things choosing you is globally positive.

People can be a fraction more difficult sometimes.

My choice, I made it as soon as I could, is perpetual summer. Coming from The North I remember waiting so long for summer to come, then remembering it for so long after it went. Cricket in Barbados and Melbourne, Rolling Stones in Hyde Park, the sweet but fleeting English summer. The Riviera is my carnival, the yacht my villa. Floats my boat.

I'd got back particularly late from Monaco. A racing driver gave me a lift home, called in for a sun upper.

I'd only been in my berth for an hour when the bells struck up. I asked to see the vicar, or whatever the correct term is, marched in, no appointment.

The young man was dressed all in black. He was the most polite man I have ever met. It would have been easier if he wasn't.

'Is there something troubling you, something you wish to tell me,' he said.

'Turn the bells off,' I said.

'Turn them off?' He seemed puzzled.

'Yes, turn them off. I can't sleep.'

'You have difficulty sleeping?' He said

I moved straight to the point.

'Turn the bells off. Please. This is for you. Call it a gift if that makes things smoother.'

He looked at the bag of euros then back at me. I couldn't read his face. A misunderstanding?

'I see,' I said. 'Look one of my people will bring you a bag exactly like this every day we are here.

The deal is you turn off the bells. We have an understanding?'

A man of God. If you can make a deal with anyone it must be him.

The next Saturday was even better than the last, if I remember rightly. Who cares? Sleep fix right through Monday.

Except my Sundays seemed to be becoming a pattern and it wasn't a dream. The bells, the bells.

I confronted the priest. 'Did you not understand me? Is it a question of money?'

The priest smiled.

'You cannot sail away from yourself,' he said.

It was years before the ringing in my ears became music and I could hear what the priest said.

'What changed?' said the racing driver. Seasons ago he'd given up life in the fast lane.

'Everything except the priest. I only went back once, saw him from afar, he hadn't aged at all. I had pushed an envelope into the offertory box. Inside were the codes to the yacht. I saw him standing on the prow conducting the choir in an al fresco acapella – *Comment te dire adieu.*'

'Do you think life is a circuit or chicane?' he asked.

Since his move to Sanary he'd replaced the steering wheel for a notebook.

I raised my glass of Bandol as the bells of Saint Nazaire embraced the harbour.

'Listen.'

SANARY

Lieu de Mémoire Vivante
Gedenkort
Memorial site

CAPITALE DE L'EXIL ARTISTIQUE ET LITTÉRAIRE
HAUPTSTADT DES KÜNSTLERISCHEN UND LITERARISCHEN EXILS
CITY OF THE ARTISTIC AND LITERARY EXILE
1933 - 1940

ERNST BLOCH	GOLO MANN
WALTER BONDY	VALERIU MARCU
BERTOLT BRECHT	LUDWIG MARCUSE
JOSEPH BREITBACH	FRITZI MASSARY
FERDINAND BRUCKNER	ANNEMARIE MEIER-GRAEFE
FRITZ BRUGEL	JULIUS MEIER-GRAEFE
FRANZ THEODOR CSOKOR	ALFRED NEUMANN
ALBERT DRACH	ROBERT NEUMANN
WILLI EISENSCHITZ	ERNST ERICH NOTH
LION FEUCHTWANGER	BALDER OLDEN
MARTA FEUCHTWANGER	ERWIN PISCATOR
BRUNO FRANK	ANTON RÄDERSCHEIDT
EMIL JULIUS GUMBEL	ERICH MARIA REMARQUE
WALTER HASENCLEVER	EMIL ALPHONS RHEINHARDT
WILHELM HERZOG	JOSEPH ROTH
FRANZ HESSEL	ILSE SALBERG
HELEN HESSEL	RENÉ SCHICKELE
LOLA HUMM-SERNAU	FRANZ SCHOENBERNER
HANS ARNO JOACHIM	LEOPOLD SCHWARZSCHILD
ALFRED KANTOROWICZ	DAVID SEIFERT
ALFRED KERR	HANS SIEMSEN
HERMANN KESTEN	HILDE STIELER
EGON ERWIN KISCH	WILHELM THÖNY
ERICH KLOSSOWSKI	CHRISTIANE GRAUTOFF-TOLLER
ARTHUR KOESTLER	ERNST TOLLER
ANNETTE KOLB	ALMA MAHLER-WERFEL
FRITZ HELMUT LANDSHOFF	FRANZ WERFEL
RUDOLF LEONHARD	FRIEDRICH WOLF
EMIL LUDWIG	CHARLOTTE WOLFF
HEINRICH MANN	KURT WOLFF
THOMAS MANN	THEODOR WOLFF
KATIA MANN	OTTO ZOFF
ERIKA MANN	ARNOLD ZWEIG
KLAUS MANN	STEFAN ZWEIG

Singular

They called the district Les Musiciens before I moved here. Now of course saves them renaming it. I wouldn't live anywhere else. Iggy Berlin, Stones London, L A Doors, me Nice. That's the way I like it.

That's the way I want it to stay.

I walk to work every day I work. If I'm not in the studio I'm by the sea, ideas come to me in waves.

Rue Berlioz is fantastic, my villa, the Faust, not as predictable as you might expect.

This cat has set himself up on the corner of Rue Karr. Main chancer.

Nothing wrong with that. I'd do the same if I had to - again. Street contact keeps you on it.

I drop him a few euros if I've had a good day before I hit Le Koncept for a cursory Kir.

He doesn't know who I am.

I expect he'll move on soon enough. Move on up, give up or make it. If he asks me for advice I'll give it, naturally, but if there is one thing I learned on my road is people have to do it their way.

It goes on for longer than I expected, him gigging on the corner I mean. I could see - hear - why it wasn't happening for him. Eventually I couldn't stop myself.

He nodded to me once when I was enroute for Le Koncept. I think it was a nod, it wasn't particularly rhythmic. Usually he was gone when I was walking back to rue Berlioz. Yeah, I may have been staying longer in the bar, the Kirs becoming precursors for something else.

'It's your singing, man,' I said. 'you're off the beat, not in a good way.'

The nodding stopped, no not rhythmic.

I was walking from the Villa to the Koncept every day now - I'd looped out the studio detour, why waste time?

One evening, he missed a beat.

'You ok, man?' He said.

I liked his speaking voice. I felt it was down to me as the older man and evidently fellow English gent to re-establish contact.

I'd kept the recording engineers on standby - you never know when the muse will return.

'Let me show you something, or rather I want you to hear something,' I said.

His guitar case was full of euros. He looked at me closely.

I smiled: 'you think I'm interested in a flight case of euros?' He didn't answer.

I offered him a beer from the studio ice box. He declined.

'Cool set up you have here, man,' He said. 'Shame you not using your time wisely.'

The impertinence threw me.

'Hit it,' I said to the duty engineer. He flicked a row of switches, the sound filled the room.

He nodded and tapped to the timing. The track stopped. He stopped. I filled the silence.

'Well?'

'You sing well,' he said.

'But.'

'Do you mind?' he said, gesturing to the engineer.

We played the track once more, laying in his guitar.

'One more time,' he said to the engineer, directly.

He played the piano in the corner of the studio. I hadn't noticed it before.

The other sound engineers rematerialized.

After the track there was silence.

The lead engineer broke it.

'He's got it,' she said, 'you've got it.'

I understood why the area was named with a plural.

Sometimes he comes down from Cimiez and we have an ice tea at the Koncept. A girl sings along to a boogie box on the corner of Alphonse Karr. We don't have time to stop.

The Smart 'Man' on the Hill

'It won't work without you, man.'

It wasn't true. No one is that indispensable but everyone likes to hear it.

I kept trying the usual – auld times sake, remember how we started, one more time- but she always said the same.

'No.'

The news bulletins were so dire these nights I was whatsapping her nearly every day.

Landslide on the Caribbean island where we recorded the third album, funding needed for latest anti-diarrhoea solution now deployed in Mali, match funding for arts centre promised for knife grime centre of East London.

'No.'

I'll be on the next TGV, change your mind.

Is there nothing I can do, nothing I can say?

The range of good causes seemed infinite, her capacity to match them with her downtime and up money correspondingly so.

She once texted me I never caused these problems, I can't solve them all.

It's true once you stop touring your currency declines but you couldn't start from a higher base.

Late at night, I must have indulged a fraction in some of the old ways, I rang her. I was hanging with one of my other clients and miscalculated the time difference.

'It's 8 o'clock in the morning.' she said 'I'm going to put the phone down now.'

I tried the 'everyone we ever knew is doing it' approach. There was the keyboard player of a prog band down with Presidents and Prime Ministers until they had to nuke his tax shelters, the lyricist who penned guilt inducing pictorials in progressive magazines until the advertisers didn't want him opposite their spreads, the saxophonist who blew into capitals addressing press conferences at aid fests from behind the fiercest of shades.

'Precisely,' she said. ' has beens, progs, jazzers, evaders, whatever. The company you keep…'

I nearly gave up. As I said, I've more clients than Jerry Macquire and the plasma screen was frozen with the atrocities streaming in across Al Jazeera, BBC World, France 24.

She said I was like the scene in the *Man Who Fell to Earth* where Bowie watches zillions of TVs at once.

I switched off the satellites and found solace in print.

Last time I saw her, kind of, was in a fading *Paris Match* I found in a stateroom of the hotel Adlon.

She was pushing a shopping trolley, more liquids than solids, through the aisles of the Carrefour Mont Boron branch. The shades and back to side baseball cap fooled no one.

It could have been so much better.

It was nearly a year later. I'd put together what we used to call a revue of unsigned bands, mid sized UK venues.

The phone went 6 AM local.

'Where are you?' she said.

I looked at the hotel information folder.

'Leeds.'

'Switch on the TV.'

It was the Promenade des Anglais. An attack on paradise, on the past, on the future. Paramedics were dashing along the front to Lenval. Pasteur 2 was stretched. The Parc Imperial was already overwhelmed.

A young doctor who slept less than we did was explaining what they needed. The list was too long for the sound bite.

'I'll be on the Jet 2, who is playing tonight?

I relayed the name.

'They've never heard of you either.' I said.

Everyone would after tonight.

Things were never the same again, for anyone.

Nice People 2018

Camera, Lights, Action

It was a technique I didn't know I'd have to perfect.

I'm not used to being in front of cameras. I'm not used to sitting in rooms alone. I'm not an actor, not a writer, but if you do this job the close up is a prerequisite to perfect.

Happens every year, Golden Bear at Kino Babylon BAFTAs at Royal Albert Hall, then Academy Awards at Dolby.

'The nominations for best director are_and the award goes to_' and then that close up as the Not You takes the length of a feature to walk to the stage. Smile, make sure it can't be construed as a grimace, clap more enthusiastically than you would for an all-seeing dictator on a podium. Stop later than the other two, leave no space for misinterpretation.

Prizes, yes I do want them, yes they do matter, it isn't merely a matter of time. I hate those peers – and that is what they are – who affect the 'who me?' schtick and 'I'm sorry I've nothing prepared.'

Until it happened to me.

It wasn't a specific project. Lifetime achievement award- subtitle, we didn't understand you at the time but we don't want you to die with nothing. Do you think this business has no heart?

It was late in the evening, the Palais was at its most bunkeresque, the wine so terrible you have to drink a lot of it to drink it.

'…the lifetime achievement award goes to_'

Then I heard my name. I kissed my leading lady and began my journey to the stand. I embraced and kissed so many on my way the red time out light was already showing when I arrived.

'I am so sorry, unexpected honour. Truly. I have no notes with me.'

You think I'm going to leave it there after so long?

Anti-climaxes are so unprofessional.

'I would like to dedicate this award to..to..' The silence wasn't intended to be dramatic. Why hadn't I seen this coming, storyboarded it out? The pause demanded an end. I never realised spots were so intense on this side. Red lights, white, the glare, the -what - radiance?

'I would like to dedicate this award to…the radiant women in our world, our business, our art, without them there is no light, if there is no light there is no cinema, there is no life…'

I never realised it was impossible to appraise your own performance. Films aren't plays, I'm no judge of applause. It did seem muted and died before I regained my seat.

'Usual?' said the chauffeur.

The atmosphere in the C6 was, - *comment vous dire* - subdued border cold. As I never imagined winning one of these awards I couldn't say what I expected but it wasn't this.

My leading lady and I never stayed in Cannes. Nice was home for us, as grounded as a pebble the tide never reaches. You should always live in a city with sea on one side.

Up coast the chauffeur opened the door for my leading lady outside La Petite Maison.

'Have a radiant evening,' he said.

The maître d showed us to our table.

'Usual?' he said to me. 'How radiant Madame looks, if I may,' he said to my leading lady.

I ordered the Bollinger 1996.

'How many glasses?' said the maître d.

Back at the Negresco my leading lady retired. I flicked around Netflix. I clicked on one of my own, research of course, not everything stands the spans of time. I clicked again.

'This content isn't working.'

There was no replacement.

'A radiant morning,' said my leading lady.

She tipped the bell girl who bought the juice and newspapers.

'So radiant.' They glanced at each other as the door was closing.

The papers were spread across the suite in an unusual order.

I had been with my leading lady every day since our wedding at a candle lit Saint Reparate a lifetime ago. It was the first time she had laid the papers out that way, from light to heavy, It was the first time we hadn't read them together, her reading aloud over the sweetening grapefruit.

'It's exquisitely radiant today,' she said, 'I'll skip the papers and fruit, might catch a socca Chez René later.'

She closed the door with a non-slam.

'*From Darkness to Light*: Pressure intensifies in Cannes.

The organizing committee of the Cannes Film Festival may be forced to reconsider its decision to award the honorary Palme d'or to one of Europe's leading film directors following allegations of his sexual misconduct. Actresses, correction actors, have emerged from the shadows to describe patterns of over tactile behaviour including hugging, unwanted embraces..'

'..A petition is gaining signatures beyond Cannes calling for the withdrawal of this years honorary Palme d'or. One actress describes how the director put his arm around her while asking her to reshoot a scene he considered unsatisfactory. I asked him to desist, she said, but he held the embrace and said my scene would be cut if I didn't do as he suggested.'

'*We are going to put your lights out*. Women object to being described as radiant. Do you think we are here to light up his world, said one leading actress?'

'Everyone will tell you, he doesn't like what you do, you end up in his arms, you have to do it again. His time is over.'

'*What a turn off*. Women don't need men to shine. The spotlight is on a new blacklist.'

'*Mr 50%?* Europe's leading film director uses his moment in the lights to praise radiant women. Did he get to where he is without men? Actors join technicians in switch off call.'

There was a knock on the door.

'You hardly need to knock darling, what do you think happened?' I said. But it wasn't her.

A woman entered, Seberg hair, YSL suit, masculin spectacles, low register voice.

'I'm sorry sir. Request from the hotel director. He is otherwise engaged this morning and cannot speak to you personally. We have no choice but to ask you to check out. The news crews outside on the promenade, their lights are disturbing our other guests. I am sure you will understand. If you would care to follow me, I am to direct you to a discreet exit.'

The Book Leaver

The way people look at me you would think I was a thief.

It is the opposite of theft. Diametric. I leave things. I leave books. On trains, trams, buses, benches, in bars, restaurants, churches. I never leave without leaving.

Why? Do you ask a thief why? Why ask me? It's a form of giving back to the universe, a research into randomness. Why not.

Started by chance. Or was it?

I was so engrossed in finishing a book I missed my stop. Dashing out I left it on the tram seat. On the street I lip read through the window people 'saying you have left this' like a pre 50 mph scene from *Speed*.

I haven't time to reread books so I simply waved.

There is always a first time. It was *No Where to Lay my Head*. Part of my non fiction period. I was walking along a street a few days later. The street was Avenue Depoilly. In the distance an object, closer, a book, closer still the title *No Where to Lay My Head*. I opened the pages, my book mark fell out.

I had found the book where the story was set.

There must be a meaning to this.

It became like the postcards in *Alone In Berlin* only in Nice after the Nazis left. I had to keep going. Leave nothing to chance.

I left *The Bay of Angels* deliberately unpropitiously at the Gare Riquier. 4 days later I stopped my Vélo Bleu along the promenade on seeing the book under the Sab Chair on the front. I checked it was my copy.

The word ' thank you' was written in fountain pen on the bookmark. I sat a while, looked around, then cycled on.

I retrieved my copy of *Super-Cannes*, deposited at the Hotel de Ville, in the business library of Sofia Antipolis.

On the Train des Pignes above the city I left Erika Mann's *Das Buch von der Riviera*. Months later I found the same copy overlooking Les Milles. 'Danke'

There must be meaning to this.

One more time: I left the *Razor's Edge* on a simple bench near St Nicholas Cathedral. On a day return to Antibes the book was on the upper deck of the Oui.SNCF. 'Thank you.'

I entered the tabac at Nice Thiers and bought a lotto.

'Lucky dip please,' I said.

I left the slip on the seat where I left the first book on the tram.

'Don't push your luck,' I said the myself, leaving a stop early, settling in the botanical garden with my anti-glare Kindle.

A stranger approached: 'sorry to interrupt,' she said factually. 'You left this on the tram. Good luck.'

Her hand had left a smudge of ink above the number 7. She noticed me notice. 'The numbers are unobscured, don't worry,' she smiled, walking away before I could thank her.

I left the reader on the bench to check the rollover.

I never saw her again.

Intra-rail

Templeton shouted the signature on my inter rail
pass book, my name as English -sounding as a vicar
calling
'Well hit, sir,'
through a mouth full of honey and tea on the chime
of 4.
Apparently.

The feeling I always knew there was something to
delayer had led me to divert to this siding, this
square.

It occurs to me how much of my life – time space
has been about places, squares, yards, quads. Place
Saint Sulpice, Masséna, Radhuspladsen, Potsdamer
Platz. Standing alone - what's new – on the
outside of this square I reflect on how these
places exist objectively.
I'm either in them or looking at them. They exist
even if I'm not there to see them, or anyone else
who was there, in these squares, platz, now, in the
immediate past, the deep past, however much of the
future is left to me. They'll exist even beyond
that, for as long as they really do exist, whether
I'm there or not, to filter, interpret. Sort of
psuedy fresher stuff you might overhear wafting up
from the quad, I know, but the traditional inter –
rail rite of passage from student daze to adulthood
was far from complete.

I look up from my passbook to the sign at the side
of me, the Hoch(high) German gothic script reminds
me of the sign in that bus station in *Where Eagles
Dare* (or some other preposterous *Victor* comic
schmaltz, the banal detail of fiction) .

I double-taked:

'Ruprecht Platz

I checked it on the old school book my mother had
given me just before I caught the first train. The
style of the handwriting inside the cover, Ilse H,
Ruprecht Platz, 1938 was not a thousand miles away
from the style of the signature in my inter-rail
book.
It made me smile, I mean, really, 1938 and all
that was so long ago smiling must be the best way
to place it this day.

The square a Viennese classic, enclosed, grey
concrete walls with windows on 4 sides. The side I
faced was the way in, a proscenium arch, above it
the wall - with the entrance gashed out - and the
windows carried on regardless.

I was standing at that point looking in. There
wasn't a way out. Particularly if you parked a 6
wheel military lorry there, crammed with rifles,
machine guns, stun grenades and other insanity to
stop the residents who might just want to saunter
out, go to the shops, post a letter; I mean it was
where they lived, the reaction rather extreme,
unfair, unsporting, I thought.

The place seemed designed for the event, that
event, some twisto architect looked into the
future, drew up a minimalist, brutalist (or is
that retro?) block of flats around one entrance to
be sealed with one lorry.

' Course it bloody upset me, must have upset
millions before me, but I could easily move on with
my circular ticket, not like all those other poor
souls with their cheap day singles which didn't
even entitle them to a seat let alone a compartment

like the ones I crashed out in on the overnighters.
Yes, alright, I confess put my feet on the seats
but no-one saw me.

I was 50% into the Inter-rail month.
London, Aachen, Brussels - decent square that -
Cologne, Lyons, Nice, Milan, Innsbruck, Vienna. If
this platz really hacked you off that basically
move it back to Nice, overnighter, step out into
the Cours Saleya, sun /bikinis /cassis, circle the
squares, get a load of that trinity.

Stuck. I could hear it all in my head, a lifetime
of tinnitus. The clack of shouldered rifles
(no, not ceremonial like that parade square
behind St James') the stupid thud of boots, the
screams of realisation, women, children, men, young
old, disabled, mentally challenged - you think I'm
going to be PC at a time like this - people being
sorted out same as I do with my recycling, tins
here, foil there, glass here.

Glass. Crystal clear. I tracked the windows now,
hysterically clean, then they must all have been
smashed.

Transfixed at that proscenium there was something
further, something not quite placed.
That was it, grey everywhere. Grey concrete, grey
window frames, even the grey chink of permitted sky
above.

Suddenly the symmetry of the closed doors was
spoiled. One old lady, ashen hair- must be 80s
passed through the door carrying a grey bucket -
didn't even have a proper watering can for Christ's
sake! - . She poured the grey water onto the one
artefact of colour in the whole place, a pot of
geraniums, the red opening with encouragement.

Time. Time to go move. Back , forward, connection
to Nice, emerge into the blue, sky, sea, girls,
aperitif time: cassis, a life full of life. My
white shirt caught the woman's eye. She moved with
surprising deftness, won our game of stare:

` Guten nachmittag, willkommen zum Platz.` Good
Afternoon, welcome to our square.

The sarcasm I learned to survive in the quad came
through by reflex –
Can't see what's bloody welcoming about this damn
place.

Yet I heard my mouth begin to tell her my name-
Templeton (it must be long after the vicar's tea
by now)

'Bitte,'- what-, the lady said.

'Templet….temp….'

She initiated a new game of stare, walk over again.
2 nil. Don't you ever learn? Game over.

'My name is Holzelmacher, I said, dredging up the
name that had drifted in from the yard to the
kitchen in my childhood semi.

'Bitte, what..?'

'Holzelmacher, my name is…'

Again the deft movement, the hand like a sticky
windscreen wiper saying , got it as soon as I saw
you.

She repeated my name, rinsed it round her mouth,
and after what seemed like 50 years, a smile

brought red to her cheeks. She must have been quite
a catch in her day.

'Wilkommen', she said, ' wilkommen zum platz.'
Welcome..back..to our square.

The geraniums were coming on nicely.

Intra -Rail *is dedicated to the Hölzelmacher family*
of Vienna.

First developed as **Squaring the Circle,** *Skyros,*
2008

Also published in the anthology
Along the Iron Veins, www.stairwellbooks.co.uk
York, 2010

Pagination for **Nice People** 6/6
2018

Down South

On the train,

Inside on a sunny day but on the move

Travelling backwards -(couldn't understand the SNCF
seat reservation system - it makes me sick)

Into a profounder France.

Turning inland, you can see your reflection in a
window

All the things that have or haven't happened since
childhood:

In the van with Mum and Dad navigating Pas de Calais
before the tunnel was even a vision

From northern England to northern France, nothing too
fancy - you have to draw the line somewhere-

To discovering the far south

The forward facing unsubmerged student with all to
play for

All in front of me until the past got me in the end.

Soundtrack in my head became so loud with what ifs
and has beens and never were's until even Holst
couldn't iPod it out.

Of course if you switch tracks there could be almost
as much in front of you as behind-

A kind of reverse hindsight

Deposit the past on the platform like a mass of
melted vinyl

Get on the right track

Out of the van and into the TGV.

Nice > Lyon, May 2010

LS 06

Pierre peered through the windscreen wipers.

 ` This is it. Junction 42. Leeds Centre and North. Our journey ends, our journey begins.'

The Rover careered on.

 ` Rain,' said Constance ` and, how do they say, chilly. We should have stayed in Nice.'

She played with the pronunciation. ` Nice, nice, Nice, nice. That's all the English ever say. Have a nice cup of tea, what a nice day…'

 'It will be as nice here,' cut in Pierre, `as it was when we came to Yorkshire for our first holiday abroad together. '

One thousand miles due south the conversation mirrored the exchange on Junction 42 but was dappled with Mediterranean sunlight.

 ` We made the right choice,' said Christine as their Citroen sped along the A8 into Nice06. I can see it, feel it, smell it.'

 ` Yes, the diesel is heavy in the air,' replied Derek with an Aznavouresque shrug.

 ` If you want to persist with the miserable northerner act that's your affaire,' said Christine. 'smell the lavender, the mimosa.'

 ` Yeah, I could murder a curry,' Derek came back. ` The thing about French food is an offal

myth, and I'm sick of the rude stares all along
this death trap auto route I've had to pay for
the privilege of driving on and…'

Christine pulled over.

    ' Right. That's enough. We are here
in Nice, full of sunny opportunities or full of
problems. Your glass is half empty of
Tetley's so aptly named Bitter, mine is half full
of Cassis. Are you in or are you out?
We both saw the advert.'

They had seen the advert. All four of them, on
their respective intranets:

" Unique opportunity – France Telecom and BT job
swap. Area Technical Manager
Leeds, Area Technical Manager Nice. 1 year
contract following two week
'find your feet' period. Support from local
accommodation agent. Don't miss out on
this chance to update your skills – professional
and cultural – and experience the good
life in two of the EU's fastest growing cities."

Christine clearly remembered Derek showing her
the advert. How he had stressed
the chance to update professional skills while
omitting it was also an opportunity to
revisit the scene of their honeymoon, 7 years
ago.

Pierre and Constance met the Leeds accommodation
agent outside the terraced house.

The agent was managing the house in " Roundhay
Park borders".

His first words to Constance were ' cheer up
love, might never happen.'

Pierre shook hands first, and tried to ignore the way the agent called his wife 'love'.

   ' All mod cons,' the man went on, 'nice and handy for the Off Licence.
Backyard's sunny as a... Sure you'll fit in nicely.'

Pierre who was so proud of his command of English language and culture began to
falter slightly. However Pierre was encouraged to see Constance warm to the surroundings. She knew the countryside they remembered was not far away.

In Nice, the agent was now an hour and a half late. Christine had chosen the café for
the meeting, just behind the promenade.

At first Christine was in her element, the elegant ladies, the Nivenesque men. Even Derek was making an effort. They ordered two glasses of Gigondas in their best French. The waiter, suave and assured, seemed
proud of his profession, unlike the bar staff back home who seemed to take your order as an insult.

   ' It's really paid off – our refresher course at Leeds Uni,' observed Christine,
' we've had no trouble ordering and these Euros are a cinch.'

   ' I'll give you that,' said Derek, his gruffness melting by the minute, ' there is one stereotype that seems to be true though, elasticity of time. Must be a lesson there for someone.
   One might expect some Latin leeway but – what is it now? – nearly two hours is overdoing it.'

As the afternoon continued Christine struggled to
reconcile Nice now with the
memory of the honeymoon there 7 years back - a
time when time didn't matter.

` Madame, monsieur, I'm Chantal, your
accommodation executive here.'

Derek stood up, `Enchanté.'

Christine had never seen Derek stand up to greet
any woman anywhere before. It was impossible not
to notice the logos on Chantal's
dress: the inevitable Hermes, the Chanel
sunglasses which stayed
on, establishing superiority over the bare eyed
Brits. Christine, her forced smile
unnoticed, waited for an apology concerning the
appointment time. It never came.

For Constance and Pierre things were progressing
positively. Over the border in
Roundhay the park was green and pleasant.
Pierre was pleased with
Constance, her efforts to integrate whenever
possible, her poise in agreeing to differ if
not, the previously undiscovered skill to chat
meaninglessly over fences. He had
always considered himself a flexible and
adaptable man but he noted with concern it
was exactly the experiences he had looked forward
to in England that were beginning
to irk him. At work all was well on the surface
but there seemed to be nothing
beyond it. He couldn't tell if the famous English
humour was funny at all but a way
of communicating something which could otherwise
never be said.

One evening a couple asked Constance and Pierre
if they ' fancied an Indian.'

     ' We'll sample the regional delicacies,'
winked Terry, his colleague. In the
restaurant Terry drank five pints of a rich,
dark beer. His wife seemed
to end every sentence with an inverted question –
don't you think, wouldn't you, isn't
it? She drank nearly as much beer as Terry.
Towards the end of the evening she said
to Pierre, ' now tell us why you really came
here. I mean why should anyone from the
south of France want to come here? There is no
reason, is there, Terry ?'

Terry asked Constance what she thought of Leeds.

     'It seems to have become so continental,' she
said. ' the shops, the pavement
cafes, direct flights to France too, I mean if we
should ever want to
go back.'

They never met the couple again socially. Pierre
always had this feeling he was at
fault. One weekend Constance took Pierre back to
the Yorkshire countryside. He
never mentioned the past, seemed preoccupied with
the future.

     ' Chantal, I asked you to come here three
days ago,' said Christine. She broke
into a sweat. She was beginning to hate the
agent, who always looked like a Lancome
advert. No one can make you feel inferior without
your consent, repeated Christine to
herself, but she couldn't help giving it to
Chantal.

Christine itemised what seemed to
her easily rectifiable jobs if someone would take
responsibility. A tap which never
quite turned off, a TV which could only pick up a
cycling channel. The incessant yap from the
poodle next door, the drip from the tap
had destabilised her. And where was Derek?

At first it was Christine who had blossomed in
Nice. She thrilled as she picked fresh
flowers every day from the old market. She became
a regular at the café off the
promenade, reflecting over a *citron pressé* how a
woman alone would never feel
comfortable in a smokey, darty, pub. Derek's
integration was more gradual
but total. Occasionally, perhaps late at night
with the crickets clicking, they
embroidered how good things were ` back home, up
north'. Then they laughed. The
list of things they missed had become shorter.
Christine even forgot that
Derek had forgotten. In 'their' café one evening
they clinked glasses and toasted ` no going
back.'

In the ladies Christine reapplied her make up in
the mirror. The fabulous art deco
frame triggered a memory. This was their
honeymoon café. She looked at her
reflection then back at the frame. The frame
hadn't changed at all.

Derek left for the office early in the morning
and returned about 9 pm. No, he didn't
want a cooked dinner. Derek's original idea of
lunch out, a Wensleydale and pickle
roll at the local, was superseded by a three
course lunch with *les*
colleagues at their adopted local restaurant. He
had become so content-inental, so
Mediterranean.

The man who before couldn't bear it if even the
slightest thing was wrong with their house now
shrugged his shoulders.

Christine heard Chantal finishing another
conditional sentence.

    ' If it wasn't - how do you say - a Bank
Holiday the day after tomorrow I
might be able to get the plumber to look at it'
and shrugged.

It was the shrug that did it. Christine was at
Nice airport within an hour.

It wasn't until she was in the taxi gliding away
from arrivals that she
began to think practically. It was the day after
the two week ' find your feet' period.

Her mobile trilled.

    ' Christine. It's Constance. I'm obliged to
give you a ring after the two week
period. Pierre and I are having a big discussion.
We went up to the Dales. Stayed in
the same hotel we were in on our first trip
abroad together.

I am saying we will never go back.

But, Pierre, he wasn't happy here. I said Nice is
crazy with crime and cars. He said if
he was going to live in a crazy city it may as
well be a sunny one. I couldn't make
him agree with his own memories. I've decided to
stay in Leeds, but Pierre is on
his way back to Nice right now! It is not a
problem for me, it may be for…'

' Constance,' smiled Christine 'people never move
back, they only go home.'

From *Wise Guy and other fables* ISBN 9780955851902 2008

Nice People 2018

I-Tone

Late summer, by the hotel pool, Juan les Pins

A : man 50's

B: woman, late 20s / 30s

The shadows are lengthening in the afternoon sun, only A and B remain on the poolside loungers.

B covered up now, wearing sarong, oversize headphones leak Caves du Roy style House.

A's dress sense slightly off, OK the linen jacket is Hackett but the sleeves up like a late series *Braquo* extra.

The music from the head phones is audible only as overflow from the headphones – this scene goes on for a long time, B moving along to her own sounds.

Eventually A puts down his Simenon novel.

A   Nice. Very handy, very handy device that, very handy.

B   NODDING ALONG , SLIGHTLY TO THE MUSIC

A   WONDERS IF IT IS WORTH TRYING AGAIN

     Handy device that. Very handy. Nice.

B   CONTINUES NODDING AND DRUMMING ALONG TO HER MUSIC

     EVENTUALLY SHE FACES HIM, WITHOUT REMOVING 'PHONES

     Yeah. Right. Very handy.

     RESUMES

...EVENTUALLY...

A   Loft. Loft, that's where they all end up. In
the end.   In the loft.

B   FACES HIM AGAIN, WITHOUT REMOVING PHONES

     Loft?

A   In the end.   In the end everything ends up there.

B   What does?

A   Vinyl. LP's, you know, vinyl. You know, just
think, imagine, everything in my loft wouldn't

     even fill your device, would hardly trouble it.
Imagine.

B   THE MUSIC CONTINUES BUT SHE PAUSES HER MOVES,
LOOKS AT HIM, STILL, FOR A LONG

     TIME. THEN RESUMES.

A   Don't mind me. I said don't mind me. No worries,
no worries at all.

B   WITHOUT STOPPING What is there to worry about?
Mint here, mint.

A   Quite. Mint. Couldn't agree more.

B   HEADPHONES OFF FOR FIRST TIME Sorry you were
saying?

A   Nothing.

B   You were saying something.

A   What? Nothing, nothing at all.

B   Just being polite, making conversation, mint
place. ' Course if you'd rather not.

A   No, nothing, nothing at all.

B   You were saying something.

      THEY FACE EACH OTHER. EVENTUALLY SHE RESUMES.

A   Handy device that. If you don't mind me saying.
Very. Handy.

New Writing original _Micro fiction_ : **I-Tone**
London, 2011

Super-Grasse

R.E.S.P.E.C.T.

Aretha always used to spell it out.

Arthur never did. He last worded you with the one word. Supermarket checkout- 'thank you, sir' 'Respect,' replied Arthur. Called to bar, 'pint for you, squire', 'Respect' said Arthur, pre-first sip.

Few people commented on it. Why do you feel the need to keep saying Respect, Arthur? Like those old communist republics who prefixed country with Democratic .

Most people didn't know what Arthur did. Those in the know knew the quiet code. Arthur wants to say Respect, be thankful.

Arthur didn't live in a talkative world. The loquacious types who did know Arthur were too dead to speak. In his circles work came to him silently. His reputation spoke for him.

Evidently a safe had not been invented which Arthur couldn't crack. Quietly. No explosives, lances, no equipment at all. Fingers, tease, focus. Respect.

He was worth his weight in gold, and Arthur was a big man.

Whatever your profession the last job comes along. The villa was nearly complete now. Arthur's choice of retirement location was classier than others in his *métier* but Arthur isn't other.

The Boss was surprisingly understanding. 'Do this last job for us, Arthur, you've earned your place on the Côte. What do you say?'

'Respect' said Arthur.

Like most professional men Arthur prided himself on his work, keeping up with the requisite continuous professional development. He called up news items in local libraries, rotating the branches so there was no discernible pattern, once twice taking the Bugatti over to the Big Library for more arcane journals.

The airless, hot working environments were rarely an issue. You wouldn't work on a unit longer than – what was the response time now – 3 minutes anyway.

Arthur agreed to mentor the new man on the team. They hadn't met before but skills need to be kept alive. It only added 41 seconds to the job, well within guidelines.

The flying squad landed on the street before Arthur and crew emerged.

'Anything you'd like to say, Arthur?' said the Chief Inspector 'of course you don't have to. We're both professionals.'

'Respect,' said Arthur.

Fin

Expatriate. Is the connotation positive or negative?
I googled it to the *OED*:

'a person living in a country that is not their own.'

I never see myself like that. I'm not frequenting
Antibes Books or the English American Library reading
test match reports in back issues of the *Telegraph*.

This is me, this is home. This is now.

Even print seems passé here. Though at least one hard
link remains.

Every Sunday morning I call in the Librarie Massena
for the international edition of *The Observer*. I take
a constitutional past the musee d'art to the Place
Arson and settle among the palms.

It is peaceful here, full of life. It was here I read
you were dead.

It wasn't an obit, it was a profile. I scanned it
first, looked up at the trajectories of the *petanca,*
then back to the page trying to make it to the end-

'Expatriate is not a term Catherine Lane ever used
about herself or others. For her the word would have
no meaning. Home is where you are, where you make it.
Did Catherine Lane herself ever make it? Again it is
a definition she would debate.

After University Lane travelled extensively. Hardly
original but at some point most people arrive. Lane
never did. A latter-day Harriet Pringle, she kept on
going. London, Toronto, Alexandria, Auckland,
Cologne, Copenhagen. It was almost as if she wanted
to collect stickers on a travel trunk and never
unpack it. Was she running from something?
Convention? Other people? Herself?

A bright young thing, she had a long run in the spreads of the heavier Sundays and Weeklies of the time. *The Listener, the New Statesman*, and of course *The Observer*. How long can you feature in columns headed New British Poets or Novelists to Watch before they tinge into What Happened to…?

The notices for her writings were most positive in the *Nouvel Observateur*, *Journal du Dimanche* and *Nice Matin*. It was in France, in Nice that she finally settled. Lane never returned to England, a country she felt misunderstood her, her life, her writing and relentlessly pursued her with the sentence of potential.

It was not, in retrospective, a literary life of the first order. She could never be compared to the Brit greats who lived among the palms – Maugham, Greene, Wells - who so belied Chekhov's maxim that Nice is a 'great place to read but a bad place to write.'

I looked up again at the delights of the square. What did these people know? I didn't want any clouds that day. I decided to read to the end. It was only an opinion.

'One can surmise how the latter years of Lane's life must have felt to her, opening the shutters onto the sea, glittering waves but no glittering prizes.

A life of potential with nothing in front a life of mediocrity with no looking back?'

Drops of rain fell on the page. I repaired to the café litterateur.

The article shocked me – why use the M word about the recently deceased? I always called words like Mediocrity bee sting words: use it to attack someone else it will harm you.

I recalled the note I sent to her when I first arrived in Nice. I had known her slightly at Goldsmiths, she was a year, maybe two above me, I wasn't sure of the etiquette.

I approached her once at a reading. She said ` when you have written three completed pieces then you can contact me.'

I was blocked 60% through the third. I told her, adding, would you like to share a *verre* with an expatriate? I'm sure it would help.'

She wrote back one word –

'Who?'

A week later she wrote again, out of the azure.

'I am sorry if my tone was abrupt and / or ambiguous I am being kind. Remember what I said. We will meet.'

I raised my glass to her. I looked again at the date of the newspaper, my manuscript finished the day she did.

Review

No Place to Lay One's Head

By

Françoise Frenkel

Paris: Gallimard 2015, London: Pushkin Press 2018

'Write a memoir as if you are writing a novel.'

This is the instruction given to students by Blake Morrison, professor of creative and life writing at Goldsmiths, University of London.

This memoir certainly contains many of the elements of a good novel, heroes and villains, vivid descriptive prose, a sense of place, tension, danger, loss, redemption.

It is, in many ways sadly, not a work of fiction. The people, the events are all too real in this past we are still connected to.

Frymeta Idesa Frenkel was born in Poland in 1889. Following University in Paris, Frenkel and her husband Simon Raichenstein set up the first French bookshop in Berlin. After the bureaucracy is negotiated the timing and location seem perfectly judged. The book shop in Charlottenburg soon became a centre of intellectual life in the German capital of the 1920s.

Gradually the times become more difficult, then sinister, then totally dangerous for a bibliophile, a foreigner, a Jew as the Nazis consolidated.

Frenkel describes her perilous flight from Berlin to Paris to Vichy. Here she finds accommodation opposite an abattoir, 'kept awake by the mournful bellowing of beasts.' By December 1940 a journey by goods train delivers her to the city of Nice.

Even here, 'against the murmuring of the sea' the situation becomes unsustainable. She presents the cast of characters residing in the 'Noah's Ark' of the Hotel la Roseraie: the Hindu prince, the anti-Nazi aristocrat from Vienna, a Republican woman from Spain, industrialists from Mannheim aiming for Palestine, earnest students and White Russians, a 'knightly' chaplain who lived by the providential maxim 'God will help us if we help each other.'

Vichy government police carry out orders with 'savage bitterness resembling joy.' Frenkel moves under increasing pressure and surveillance to the hills of the Alpes-Maritime, finally held in a vicious regime in a detention centre in Annecy.

The story ends abruptly with a desperate escape over the border to Switzerland in June 1943.

It is only through the chronology published in the afterword of the Pushkin Press edition that we learn that the author returned to Nice probably at the end of 1945 and lived there until her death in 1975.

There is no mention in the text of Simon Raichenstein. An editorial footnote reveals his name is inscribed on the Shoah Memorial in Paris, with date and place of death given as Auschwitz-Birkenau 19 August 1942.

No Place to Lay One's Head prompts interesting literary considerations apart from Prof Morrison's dictum above. Do we need to know more about the author other than what is found in the manuscript? In the preface Nobel Prize laureate Patrick Modiano thinks not –

'Do we really need to know more? I don't believe we do. What makes *No Place to Lay One's Head* unique is that we cannot precisely identify its author. This eyewitness account of the life of a woman hunted through the south of France and Haute-Savoie during the Occupation is more striking in that it reads like the testimony of an anonymous woman, much as *A Woman in Berlin* – also published in Switzerland in the 1950s – was thought to be for a long time.'

The story is essentially a triptych of time and place, each presented as a living picture. The intellectual epicentres of Paris and Berlin before Nazis conflagrate creativity, Nice, and the struggle for life itself in the Franco-Swiss border region.

The vibrancy of Berlin is portrayed from the inside. It is overcome by a gradualism of bureaucrats and thugs until Nazism becomes a total system of nihilism.

Frenkel joins other artists including Jean Vigo, Raoul Mille, Winston Graham, Graham Greene, Robert Kanigel and Ronald Frame who express the glittering surface of Nice and the darkness beneath.

Juxtapositions continue into the final sequence on the border between Nazi controlled France and neutral Switzerland. Frenkel meets people who are kind and selfish, brave and self-serving, honest and deceitful. People who carry out orders, people who don't.

To us many of these dualities seem depressing, why did the vibrant capital city decline, the abundant city by the sea fall so low, the civilised bookseller become almost annihilated by barbarism?

Contemporaneous reflections, concisely and often visually told, resonate across time. Hitler is a leader with the face of an automaton. News, from whatever media, can be everything and nothing.

In Avignon the radio is less ubiquitous than Paris but the realities of war in the north are inescapable. 'Poland, Denmark, Belgium, Holland, all these invaded countries were like pieces of the planet that had been wrenched off, with no hope of contact, and only infrequent and distant signs of devastation and suffering were still making their way through to us.'

There is a touch of almost surreal irony in the dossier attached at the end of the publication. A suitcase left in Champs-Élysée storage depot in May 1940 is immaculately itemised by the Gestapo in November 1942 on seizure of the property 'on grounds of race.' In 1960 Frau Frenkel receives compensation of 3500 DM from the Federal Republic of Germany.

Ultimately the writer conveys a sense of triumph, the route of the journey we take with her essentially positive.

She wrote on the original manuscript cover deposited in Lyon Municipal Library in 1945

'I seek inner peace: I am grieving for so many and know not where my family have been laid to rest.' A notice in the record of publications received states 'rays of light illuminate the images of misery, and for that we must be grateful to the author. There are no complaints, just facts, reported with a sense of decency and in a measured but most lively fashion.'

It is fitting to conclude with Frenkel's own foreword-

'it is the duty of those who have survived to bear witness to ensure the dead are not forgotten, nor humble acts of self-sacrifice left unacknowledged. May these pages inspire a reverent thought for those forever silenced, fallen by the wayside or murdered. I dedicate this book to the men and women of goodwill who, generously, with unfailing courage, opposed the will to violence and resisted to the end.'

W

Review for *Second Generation Voices* 69

ISSN 2397-5016

www.secondgeneration.org.uk

>Nice People 2018

Also by John F King at York Europe Publishing:

Wise Guy and other fables, 2008

ISBN 978-0-955851902

Wise Guy, 2012, is also available as an eBook at

Smashwords ISBN 9781476351735

*Drama King, 2010

ISBN 978-0-955851919

Funky / Guy and other micro-fiction, 2012

ISBN 978-0-955851964

Micro-Waves, 2012

ISBN 978-0-955851933

Vienna, Love, 2014

ISBN 978-0-955851971

Write_Coach, 2014

ISBN 978-0-955851988

Write_Coach II 2015

ISBN 978-0-9931306-1-8

A and E   2014

ISBN 978-0-955851995

Prog 2015

ISBN 978-0-9931306-0-1

What's Left 2016

ISBN 978-0-993106-2-5

Low – Rise 2016

ISBN 978-0-9931306-3-2

SW10 2017

ISBN 978-09931306-4-9

West End Story 2018

ISBN 978-0-993106-5-6

www.ingramcontent.com/pod-product-compliance
Lightning Source LLC
Chambersburg PA
CBHW071210130626
46555CB00004B/1647